D1631873

A MESSAGE FROM CLOUDBASE

Hello, Colonel White here. Welcome
to this special bulletin issued by
S.P.E.C.T.R.U.M. In the following
pages you will find details of
Spectrum Personnel and craft. The
information is highly sensitive and
is for your eyes only. One thing you
must remember:

CAPTAIN SCARLET IS INDESTRUCTIBLE -

YOU ARE NOT!

We at Cloudbase hope you find the
following interesting and enjoyable.

HEAR US EARTHMAN

£4.75

CAPTAIN SCARLET
AND THE
MYSTERONS
ANNUAL

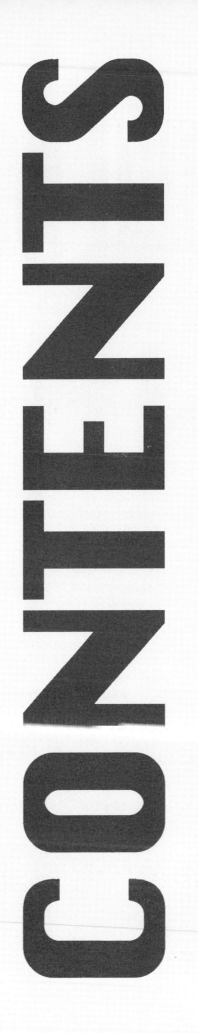

CONTENTS

Published by Grandreams Ltd
Jadwin House
205-211 Kentish Town Road
London NW5 2JU

Printed in Italy

THIS IS
SPECTRUM

THE YEAR is 2065. The world is by no means at peace as civil wars and bandit-run governments create instability on Earth and beneath the seas.

Yet the greatest threat to our planet comes from outside the atmosphere. Unexplained and uncontrolled, the Mysterons have declared war on Earth's citizens.

The world is run by the World Government, a powerful, democratic organisation that represents 95 per cent of the Earth's individual states and territories. Before the danger from the Mysterons became known, it had been decided to set up a special force whose priority was to keep the peace. The new security organisation was designed to relieve the pressure from the existing World Government defence groups. This force became know as Spectrum.

Personnel had to be drafted and a permanent base established. World Government departments and services provided a reservoir of trained and dedicated people, so the Spectrum staff were relatively easy to recruit, but equipment and installations had to be of a highly specialised nature - custom-built for the new force.

Ideas were formulated under the guidance of a Select Committee and the location of the all-important headquarters was debated. The base's construction and its

ultimate location had, for security reasons, to remain secret.

At first it was hoped to shape this massive headquarters into a submarine craft to float beneath the deep Pacific Ocean, but this was ruled out because of the large number of hostile underwater inhabitants. A floating island was suggested, but this was eventually thought to be impractical and was rejected. Next, a land based complex in the Sahara Desert or the Amazon Jungle was considered, but the risk of publicity was too great.

The committee enthused about the headquarters being housed in a space station in Earth-orbit, but this idea was ruled out too, because of budget factors and

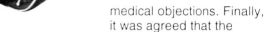

medical objections. Finally, it was agreed that the operations of Spectrum should be conducted from a self-propelled, free floating platform located somewhere in the upper atmosphere some 15,000 metres above sea level.

Contracts for the construction were put out to tender... not to one organisation, but to a host of small specialised industrial concerns scattered across the globe. Security was the watchword and the individual companies were unaware of the final design of the complex. Weeks passed and equipment

began to be delivered to receiving stations dotted about the world.

Eventually the equipment was shipped to a collecting centre in Sweden where the ultimate construction of the headquarters, later to become known as Cloudbase, was determined. The components were assembled in a huge underground site specially designed for World Government security projects. Cloudbase was put together in fifty prefabricated sections to await final construction in outer space.

Over a dozen space-ferry freighters took off and journeyed to the edge of the Earth's atmosphere to rendezvous with a deserted weather control space station where their cargoes were 'parked'. A specially selected construction team had taken over occupancy of the weather satellite, and soon the work began.

Enjoying zero-gravity, the team built the headquarters in outer space in a very short time. Then, with a full complement of just under 600 personnel aboard, Cloudbase moved under its own power back into the Earth's atmosphere to begin its activities as the Spectrum Control Centre.

Meanwhile, on Earth, personnel were being screened for the key jobs of Spectrum Agents. Ten people were finally selected, each being given a code name that related to a colour. The World Government chose a Universal Secret Service agent to head up the Spectrum organisation. He was Charles Grey, later code named Colonel White.

Ninety people were sent with the ten agents to take part in rigorous training, and these individuals were given the less glamorous, yet most essential positions on Cloudbase.

Five female pilots made up the strike squadron, later to become the Angels; a medical officer was chosen, the best there was in the world, Dr. Fawn, and finally a communications genius was selected, Lieutenant Green.

The hundreds of personnel who had been turned down as staff for Cloudbase headquarters were still employed by Spectrum. They were given new identities and

a new country of origin and were scattered about the world. Their job was to gain official standing and acceptance in their chosen community in whatever position - tramp, millionaire, shop-keeper - anything that would give them an undercover position and be ready to help Spectrum function smoothly.

Spectrum was ready, and for the short time it operated as a security force, its results were outstanding. But with the changing times, the World was threatened by an unknown force called the Mysterons. There was now urgent need for a super strike and protection force to challenge and fight the deadly menace from outer space.

Due to its proven efficiency, the specialisation of its equipment, and the effectiveness of its staff and agents, the Spectrum organisation was needed to - save the world from the threat of the Mysterons.

TESTS ARE IN OPERATION ON A NEW AND HIGHLY *COMPLEX* TYPE OF LINK-UP BETWEEN SPACE CAPSULES...

THE NEWLY DEVELOPED ELECTROMAGNO DEVICE GUIDES THE TWO CAPSULES TOGETHER...

EARTH CONTROL LOSES CONTACT...

CONTROLS DAMAGED, TWIN TWO STARTS TO OVERHEAT ON ITS RE-ENTRY PATH...

SUDDENLY THE TWO CAPSULES COLLIDE...

CONTROLLER TO TWIN ONE. WHAT IS THE FAULT?

HAVE REGAINED CONTROL OF CAPSULE! AM ON RE-ENTRY PATH! CAN'T SEE WHAT'S HAPPENED TO TWIN TWO!

THIS IS THE VOICE OF THE MYSTERONS WE KNOW YOU CAN HEAR US *EART*

TWIN TWO CAPSULE EXPLODES IN A BLINDING FLASH...

THEN SUDDENLY APPEARS ONCE MORE...COMPLETE IN EVERY DETAIL...

THE CAPSULES LAND AT CAPE KENNEDY SPACEPORT...

ASTRONAUTS, GARY PORTER AND BLAKE CAMPBELL WALK AWAY...

THE LINK-UP FAULT IS GONNA SET PROJECT PLUTOS BACK A COUPLE OF MONTHS, CAMPBELL!

YEH... THE CONTROLLER WON'T BE HAPPY!

THE WORLD GOVERNMENT SPACE ADMINISTRATOR WILL DIE TOMORRO...

HOVERING HIGH ABOVE EARTH, THE SPECTRUM ORGANISATION ACTS INSTANTLY...

GET A TAB ON THE ADMINISTRATOR, LIEUTENANT GREEN!

I HAVE, SIR. HE'S IN MIAMI. TOMORROW HE VISITS CAPE KENNEDY!

MIAMI AIRPORT...

ALL SET, CAPTAIN GREY?

S.I.G. CAPTAIN SCARLET! THE ADMINISTRATOR IS STAYING AT THE NAUTILUS HOTEL!

NEXT DAY, SPECTRUM COLLECTS THE ADMINISTRATOR AND HEADS FOR CAPE KENNEDY...

CAPE KENNEDY SPACEPORT

AT CAPE KENNEDY...

DELAYS! DELAYS! WHAT WENT WRONG YESTERDAY?

I SUGGEST WE ALL GO TO THE PROJECT HANGER WHERE I CAN EXPLAIN. ASTRONAUTS CAMPBELL AND PORTER ARE ALSO THERE!

THIS IS THE VOICE OF THE MYSTERONS

SPECTRUM

NAME: CAPTAIN SCARLET

PERSONNEL

Born in Winchester, England, 17 December 2036, Captain Scarlet's real name is Paul Metcalfe and he is Spectrum's number one agent.

With a family background steeped in military tradition - his father, grandfather and great-grandfather all served with distinction in the World Army - it was natural for Paul, after graduation from Winchester University, to decide on a military career.

Enrolling at West Point Military Academy, USA, Metcalfe soon found himself under the ruthless regime which was to turn him into a top rank combat soldier.

Instead of taking a commission, Paul decided to enlist in the World Air Force. By the time he was twenty-four, he had seen active service in many parts of the world where leadership, courage and professional ability won him promotion to full colonel - and the attention of the Spectrum selection board.

Metcalfe was approached and offered the rank of Captain with full privileges, and the code name Scarlet.

The incredible story of his Mysteronisation, death and revival by Spectrum's surgical team, proves beyond doubt that Captain Scarlet is indestructible! This incredible fact means that Scarlet is vital in the war against the Mysterons.

SPECTRUM SPV

VEHICLES

SPECTRUM PURSUIT VEHICLE

Estimated speed: 200 mph

Length: 7.62 metres

Brakes: Magnetic disc reverse thrust

Steering: By cylindrical Hydropneumatics

Power unit:
Land: **Front wheel drive, hydrogenic electrical fuel cells**
Water: **Twin aqua-jets mounted at rear**

Fast, armed, armoured and amphibious, the S.P.V.s constitute Spectrum's major Earth-bound combat vehicles. Because of the complexity of design and equipment these vehicles have to be specially hand-built at secret locations in top security hangars. There is no windscreen: the driver sits in an aircraft type bucket seat facing the rear and drives with the aid of video/monitor systems.

Carried on the vehicles are revolutionary radar installations, super sensitive transceiver radio equipment, and a proteinised food supply. A built in air-conditioning plant allows the S.P.V. to cope with any emergency.

The power unit is detachable, and held in position by twin clamps, it is coupled independently to all road wheels. When the power unit is detached and being used for such purposes as personnel thrust-pack, ancillary minor propulsion unit etc, stand-by batteries provide the S.P.V.'s driving force.

At the rear of the vehicle are fitted two caterpillar tracks, enabling the vehicle to climb all but vertical objects and terrain.

The S.P.V.'s armament consists of laser cannons, ground-to-air missiles and electrode ray cannons - the only effective anti-Mysteron weapon.

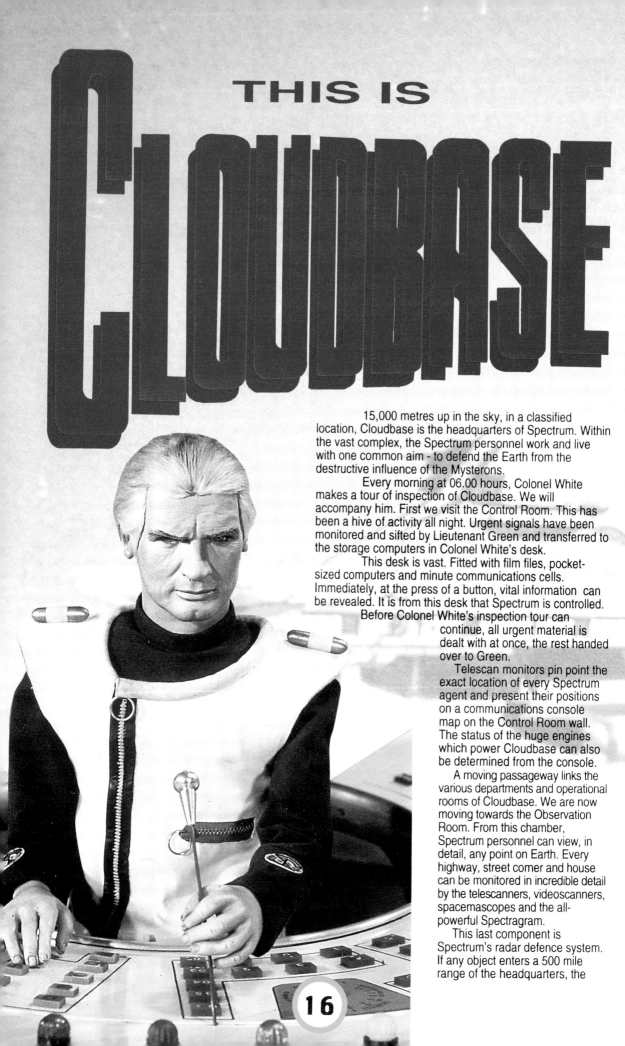

THIS IS CLOUDBASE

15,000 metres up in the sky, in a classified location, Cloudbase is the headquarters of Spectrum. Within the vast complex, the Spectrum personnel work and live with one common aim - to defend the Earth from the destructive influence of the Mysterons.

Every morning at 06.00 hours, Colonel White makes a tour of inspection of Cloudbase. We will accompany him. First we visit the Control Room. This has been a hive of activity all night. Urgent signals have been monitored and sifted by Lieutenant Green and transferred to the storage computers in Colonel White's desk.

This desk is vast. Fitted with film files, pocket-sized computers and minute communications cells. Immediately, at the press of a button, vital information can be revealed. It is from this desk that Spectrum is controlled.

Before Colonel White's inspection tour can continue, all urgent material is dealt with at once, the rest handed over to Green.

Telescan monitors pin point the exact location of every Spectrum agent and present their positions on a communications console map on the Control Room wall. The status of the huge engines which power Cloudbase can also be determined from the console.

A moving passageway links the various departments and operational rooms of Cloudbase. We are now moving towards the Observation Room. From this chamber, Spectrum personnel can view, in detail, any point on Earth. Every highway, street corner and house can be monitored in incredible detail by the telescanners, videoscanners, spacemascopes and the all-powerful Spectragram.

This last component is Spectrum's radar defence system. If any object enters a 500 mile range of the headquarters, the

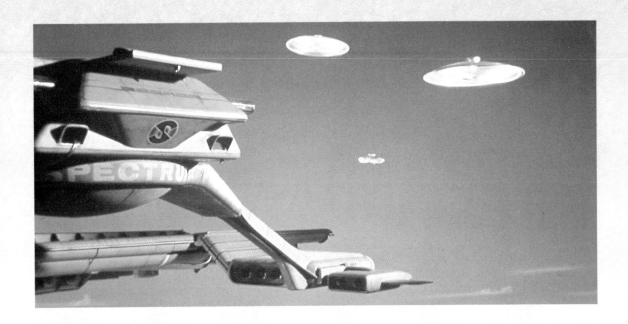

Spectragram will register and immediate action will be taken.

Through observation tubes, transparent-walled tunnels through which can be seen the clouds around Cloudbase, and the massive deck spreading below to right and left, the size of a dozen football pitches.

Escalators, ventilated from above, lead down from the main control centre and flight deck to the lower decks of Cloudbase. The Amber Room, decorated in restful pastel shades, is the stand by bay for the Angel pilots. It is here the Angels wait for their orders, relaxing

hold it for a few moments in suspension, until it is allowed to gently touch-down on the deck.

At 08.00 hours, the tour of inspection is nearly complete. There is one final stop - the engine rooms.

Massive control panels greet us as we enter the vast complex on the lower deck of Cloudbase. Control panels are arranged from the ground to meet the ceiling, complemented with many hundreds of dials and flashing lights. Here a control supervisor sits. A button is pressed and he pin-points the vast detailed engineering components that make up each engine. Details are flashed across the monitor screens and

with the many books, videos, films and tapes stored in the most sophisticated entertainment system built within the walls of the room.

From the Amber Room, the Angels can be quickly transported along glass chutes directly into their aircraft in the hangar above.

Beneath the flight deck, Colonel White gets a report of the readiness of the three sleek strike aircraft which are the main line of attack for Cloudbase. Technicians with computerised robot assistance make sure everything is in top working order. Every forty-eight hours, the craft are changed over, ensuring perfect operating conditions at all times.

Once more into the elevator, we follow Colonel White up towards the flight deck. The conditions are considered, go for a stroll on the flight deck, and donning respirator equipment and insulated pressure suits, we step onto the cold, almost airless deck. Stretching before us lies the perfect runway. Here, the first piece of equipment visible is the Spectrafan. Lifted into position by hydraulic elevators, the fan is so effective that the pressure it generates can stop an approaching aircraft dead in its tracks, then

scanners automatically programme the computers for an on-the-spot maintenance check

If a malfunction is shown, it can be localised and dealt with immediately. Each control panel and function is duplicated in case of failure...nothing is left to chance.

There are over twenty engines in this room providing power for the many life-support systems, energy requirements and propulsion operations of Cloudbase. A separate control panel monitors the status of the four giant hover combines that keeps Cloudbase moored in position.

These work by air being sucked into the engines and pressurised to create a fantastic force. When the pressure reaches the required standard it is forced through a gridwork of ducts. The air rushes downwards, enabling the headquarters to remain stable.

The tour is complete. Now the real work of the day begins...the continuous fight against the Mysteron threat.

WE, THE MYSTERONS, SHALL RELEASE TWO THOUSAND RUTHLESS CRIMINALS

THE WALL of green sea folded. Countless tons of water fell, spread, exploded and foamed over the stern deck of the ten-acre fishing platform. This was the eye of a Pacific storm. There was no sky between the towering wave crests, and the cascades of rain and spume rattled the deck and stung the flesh of men as if they had been hit by grapeshot.

There was very little light, although it was noon, just enough for the stern deck officer to see one of the small boats swinging in its davits like a shop sign.

"Stern deck damage team..secure number twelve!" He spoke sharply into the small microphone.

A few moments later five men in yellow survival suits hauled themselves hand over hand along the nylon deck lines towards the davit. Trapped water slopped around their ankles. Three times before they reached the dangling boat, green water rushed across the deck, foaming around their waists.

The small power-boat swung hard against the davits as the men reached it. One man grabbed its gunwale to hold it steady and called the others to help. They had seen another green wave tumbling like an avalanche across the deck and were hugging the life-lines to save themselves.

The water hit the man and the power-boat, battering them out to the lee, swirling, swamping and burying them. The floating

platform rose slowly. The men on the life-lines looked at the empty davits, the empty pulley blocks and the shreds of rope flapping and cracking in the gale.

Man and boat had gone.

Frank Osborne died, but his death in that sea had been noticed by that evil intelligence, the Mysterons. They took Frank Osborne, restored him to life and set him back upon the deck. He looked and spoke like Frank Osborne, but he thought and acted as his eerie masters willed - as a Mysteron agent.

Frank Osborne was ordered to the sick bay for a medical check. The check was detailed and thorough, and he was left alone on the couch when the doctor and the male orderly both went into the annex to consult the computerised symptom analyser.

Frank Osborne rose from the couch, lifted a pint jar of ether from the dispensary shelf and stepped silently out into the companionway. Three doors along he knew he would come to a cabin crammed with electronic apparatus.

This was the control unit of the platform's steering system.

Osborne emptied the ether about the room. The fluid vapourised swiftly in the warm air, which fast became unbreathable. Osborne felt for a pair of wires that linked two sections of the complicated apparatus! He pulled them. They tore from their connections with an electrical spark. The ether exploded, the room shattered. Fire alarms clanged, and the fire fighting teams ran to their positions. One officer rushed to check the steering systems room from where the fire alarm had originated. But he found it normal. He reported, "False alarm!"

The Mysterons had destroyed the complex

system and re-created it so that it would obey their will, their commands alone.

The doctor checked on Frank Osborne. He was lying on the couch, just as he had left him.

"Tonight the western coast of America will be a region of fear and terror, for we, the Mysterons, shall release two thousand ruthless criminals!"

"How are they going to do it, Colonel White?"

"That's exactly what I want you to ask your computers, Lieutenant Green."

"Very good, sir, but there is very little information to go on, so far," replied the Spectrum lieutenant, as he propelled his chair from one end to the other of the glass and printed-circuit complex that was the mechanical grain of Spectrum, the world security organisation engaged in mortal battle with the Mysteron menace.

"Check on all confinement centres in the Western States of America."

"There's nothing, Sir," the young officer from Trinidad replied, glancing up from the computer. "There's no prison with more than two hundred occupants, and to release two thousand men would entail at least fifteen separate prison break-out operations."

Continued on page 28

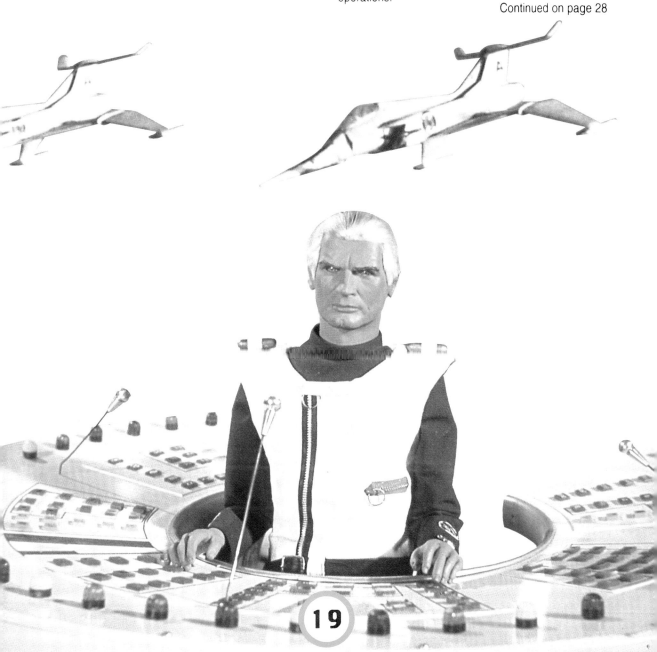

SPECTRUM SSC

SALOON CAR

Estimated speed: 150 mph
Length: 5.5 metres
Bodywork: Fleetonium
Brakes: Electro-magnetic reverse thrust

Power unit: Compressed gas turbine driving front and rear wheels
Armament: Standard Spectrum rapid fire small arms.

The Spectrum Saloon Car provides high speed mobility for Spectrum personnel. Designed to Spectrum specifications, incorporating speed and safety, this car is capable of carrying five persons. All cars are fitted with special transistorised ultra high frequency transceiver radios maintaining constant contact with Cloudbase and the Angels.

The new lightweight, resilient Fleetonium is used in the bodywork construction. The rear floor raises to give mechanics access to the gas turbine situated below. Hot gas from the combustion chamber drives compressor and power turbines before being ejected through the rear grill. All wheels are sprung independently.

The lighting system is designed to cater for all eventualities; it includes an infra-red beam with detector eye, quartz headlights and a long distance viewing laser projector with optical telescope, which is coupled to a video screen in the cabin.

Sidelights and trafficators are of the non-failing design incorporated by the World Motor Manufacturers early in the 21st century. Braking is by special magnetic brake drums where opposing magnetic fields are generated by means of electromagnets.

WE ARE THE

MYSTERONS

"WE THE MYSTERONS SHALL DESTROY..."

The spine-chilling message that haunts the Earth and echoes through Cloudbase has its origins and source in the heart of the Mysteron complex - headquarters of the greatest enemy the world has ever know. For the Mysterons have discovered the power of completely reversing the process of destruction, so making any object almost exactly as it was before, the only difference being that once Mysteronised, the object is under the control of the Mysterons.

As no Earthman has ever been inside the city, it is impossible to give any factual information concerning the Mysterons. One theory put forward is that there is now no race of beings in the complex - only programmed computers.

Although this answers many puzzling aspects of the Mysteron attacks on Earth, many

Spectrum scientists discount it because it suggests that the mechanical computer has been given an illogical emotion - and that is considered to be impossible.

What facts we do know are that Captain Black, on a mission in a Martian exploration vehicle, one of the Zero X series, assumed the worst when he came upon what is now considered to be the Mysteron complex. He ordered the complete destruction of the city, and the computers reacted at once. The Mysterons swore vengeance on the Earth. Captain Black was killed and reconstructed - or Mysteronised - to become the Mysterons' Earth-based agent.

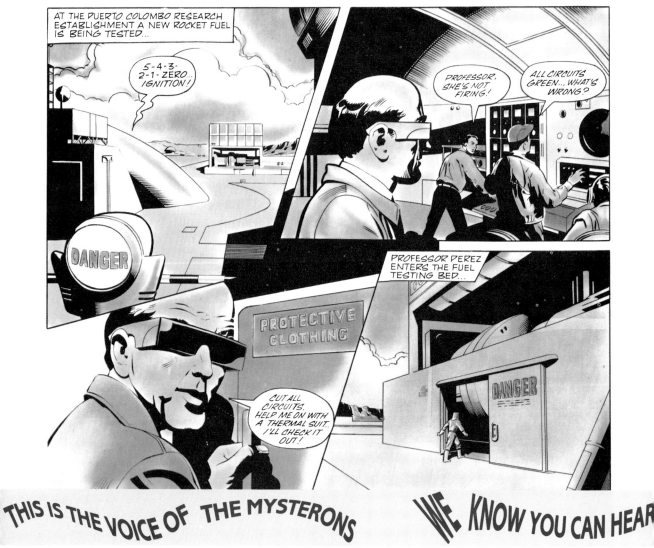

SCARLET MAKES A DESPERATE BID...

MEANWHILE...

TURBINE CONTROL FROM BLUE. CAPTAIN SCARLET HAS INTERCEPTED MYSTERON AGENT!

AS THE LIFT COMES TO A HALT, SCARLET DELIVERS THE LAST BLOW... QUICKLY HE OPENS THE TOOL BAG...

IN THE CONTROL ROOM...

EMPTY...HE'S PLANTED THE FUEL...AND I'VE LOST MY MOUTH MIC... THERE'S NO WAY TO WARN THEM...

TURBINE 4... OPEN!

FOOL! WE'RE OPENING THE TURBO SLUICE-GATES NOW TO COINCIDE WITH THE PRESIDENT'S OPENING SPEECH IN VALPARAISO!

SPECTRUM HAS FAILED...

SOMETIMES I THINK THE MYSTERONS WILL SUCCEED IN DESTROYING US ALL!

THAT'S WHAT THEY WANT YOU TO START THINKING, CAPTAIN. BUT THEY'LL NEVER BEAT US COMPLETELY... NEVER!

THIS IS THE VOICE OF THE MYSTERONS

SPECTRUM

PERSONNEL

NAME: COLONEL WHITE

Supreme Commander in Chief of Spectrum, Colonel White is the major factor in Earth's security. Born 14 July, 2017, London, England, Colonel White's real name is Charles Gray. He was educated at King's College, Canterbury, and Norwich University, and gained first class honours in computer control, navigation and technology. On graduation, White entered the British Navy. He soon proved his ability.

Service in destroyers, submarines and JTB's in such trouble spots as S.E. Asia in 2040, the Iceland dispute in '42, the Panama Isthmus rebellion in '42-43 left him a young veteran of many campaigns.

Eventually becoming Admiral of the Fleet, Gray surprised the world when he suddenly announced his retirement - but only to camouflage the next step in his career. He became a key member in the Universal Secret Service. After two years as a U.S.S. agent, he was promoted to the Organisation and Control Section.

As head of the British Corps of the U.S.S. he turned a disorganised collection of agents from inefficient despair to a compact fighting machine. Now, as first head of Spectrum, he faces the toughest task of his career.

NAME: DOCTOR FAWN

Yalumba, Australia, is where Edward Wilkie was born on 10 July, 2031, now code named Doctor Fawn, whose job on Spectrum is Supreme Medical Commander of Cloudbase.

The son of a prominent Australian specialist, it seemed inevitable that Fawn should take up his father's career and become a doctor.

After a brilliant university career at Brisbane, he joined the World Medical Organisation, where he continued to dumbfound his superiors with his outstanding ability and his specialisation in computer assisted medical research.

Promoted to Health Controller for Scandinavia he was then given control of the vital Advancement of Medicine and Medical Science Division.

When Spectrum began their recruitment for Cloudbase, Doctor Fawn was the immediate choice. He accepted without hesitation.

SPECTRUM MSV

MAXIMUM SECURITY VEHICLE

Estimate speed: 200 mph
Length: 7.31 metres
Weight: 8128 kilos
Power unit: Front: Transverse 8 cylinder rotary diesel
Rear: Transverse coupled 8 cylinder rotary diesel
Wheels: Four sets of double wheels fitted with bullet-proof self-inflating tyres

Designed to carry four persons in complete security and comfort, the M.S.V. is hand built by expert coach builders. It is claimed to be indestructible after exhaustive tests by the World Army and Air Force under severest battle conditions.

As with all Spectrum vehicles, it is fitted with advanced radar, video, transceiver radios and is complete with survival food kit.

Designed specifically to carry threatened VIPs in the utmost safety, it is also an exceptional combat vehicle armed with laser cannons and anti-Mysteron electrode ray cannons.

If the M.S.V. is in any area after a nuclear attack, it is immediately hermetically sealed to all outside contact, having its own pressurised air-filtration plant. Solar collector strips are fitted to the vehicle for recharging the batteries used to drive the stand-by motor. Hydraulic-clamped link suspension holds the twin wheels which have power steering. The maximum security windows are fitted with special heat-resistant anti-radiation lead quartz.

Main construction is of high intensity armour-plated steel, with refrigeration honeycomb and radiation damping sandwich. Suspension is of the hydraulic clamped link classification, being independent to all wheels.

WE, THE MYSTERONS,

White. "That's a floating prison colony engaged in sea harvesting. And you say it's adrift?"

Lieutenant Green nodded.

"Then, that's it! Despatch Angels on a search and report mission to the area. Get Captains Scarlet and Blue up here!"

Colonel White's first order was passed to the Amber Room and within seconds three high-speed delta-wing aircraft had been fired from the flight deck of Cloudbase. The three girl pilots formed a tight arrow head formation and turned on a supersonic course to the north Pacific Ocean.

"Harmony Angel from Melody Angel... I've a blip reading on bearing seven seven two... it could be what we're searching for, honey!"

"Melody from

Continued from page 19

The colonel frowned and leaned his elbows on his circular desk. "That doesn't fit the usual methods employed by the Mysterons. They usually strike by means of one single operation. Check wider, lieutenant."

"Here's something, colonel," Green called. "The Oregon Banks fishing platform has reported steering difficulties... and it is in a force ten gale."

"The Oregon Banks platform," said Colonel

Harmony...close and verify visually... Symphony Angel orbit with me at five thousand feet."

The powerful aircraft manoeuvred according to instructions. Before long Melody reported that she had found the huge fishing raft. It was rolling in the cross-currents on the edge of the gale.

News of the girl's find was reported to Spectrum control in Cloudbase.

Colonel White permitted himself a grim smile.

"This is the one," he said sourly to Captain Scarlet. "That fishing platform houses two thousand hardened violent criminals, each one a menace to law-abiding society. This is why they are sent to work on that fish harvesting platform, so that they can be employed on productive work, whilst under maximum security conditions."

"Normally it is impossible to escape from a platform floating in the ocean," said Scarlet. "But now the Mysterons have taken a hand to make it possible."

"And think of the trouble that will be caused if two thousand desperate men are suddenly released on the West Coast. There will be violence and mayhem. Honest citizens will live in fear. Police and civil authorities will be stretched to the limit in rounding up that number of criminals. Some may never be recaptured."

"Are the warders still in charge?" asked Captain Blue.

Colonel White snorted. "That's anybody's guess now," he said. "The last radio signal from the platform reported an outbreak on one of the lower level detention decks. It appears that a maximum security warder was overpowered. Before the culprit could be apprehended he managed to release a whole group of prisoners. Since then there has been silence."

Captain Scarlet had been thinking hard for the last few seconds. He spoke sharply. "It's my hunch that as yet there are only one or two Mysteron agents aboard that platform, and that they have Mysteronised only part of the machinery - the steering control. There would have been no need to take over the entire construction. It would be a spectacular thing to do, and would certainly have been noticed."

"Okay, so how does that hunch help us? The platform is still nearing the West Coast with two thousand desperate men aboard," White said.

"I've thought of a plan," Scarlet replied. "It is a dangerous one that only I can undertake. My objective will be to reach the Mysteronised steering control computers, and not only cut them out of the platform's circuitry, but also cut them entirely from the vessel itself. The Mysterons can re-create anything that has been destroyed...but they can do nothing if it has merely been removed."

The Spectrum helicopter skimmed the crests of the heaving waves. The central fury of the storm had passed, but the aftermath still troubled and tossed the deep green waters.

Zero altitude was dangerous flying. Thin white crusts of salt already stained the underside of the aircraft. There was the ever present danger that an extra large wave would rise and break, catching the aircraft and drag it out of the air.

They first glimpsed the huge platform rising out of the sea half a mile away. They saw little more than its massive outline and glistening superstructure before high waves and a squall blocked all sight.

Captain Blue adjusted his course. As he did so he glanced at his co-agent Captain Scarlet.

"Are you ready?" he asked.
"Ready!"

Captain Blue flew the helicopter in fast. The fishing platform was in sight again, towering fifty feet above wave height. He hovered alongside, a few feet above a porthole, matching the rise and fall of the platform.

He looked at Captain Scarlet who was standing in the open hatch, two metal cylinders strapped to his back and other equipment buckled around his waist.

Scarlet jumped.

He felt cold winds catch and buffet him. He thrust out the magnetic clamps he held in each hand. They clanged and dragged as they made contact with the side of the platform's hull, and suddenly they held firm. Scarlet brought his legs against the metal plating, and similar pads on his knees and toes held tight.

Continued on page 44

THE SPECTRUM

PERSONNEL

RHAPSODY:
Real name: Dianne Simms, born 22 April, 2043, London

HARMONY:
Real name: Chan Kwan, born 19 June, 2042, Tokyo

MELODY:
Real name: Magnolia Jones, born 10 January, 2043, Georgia, U.S.A.

DESTINY:
Real name: Juliette Pontoin, born 23 August, 2040, Paris

SYMPHONY:
Real name: Karen Wainwright, born 6 January, 2042, Iowa, U.S.A.

The five beautiful women who make up the Angel's team form the most deadly air-combat fighting force of the century. Uniformly qualified in flying experience, danger and intellect, the Angels are a stern reminder to the World Government's enemies of Spectrum's retaliatory powers.

To achieve the full potential of the supersonic jet craft flown by the Angels demands the highest degree of flying skill. The pilots exceed these requirements.

When off duty, the Angels relax in the Amber Room on Cloudbase where a comprehensive library of books together with the most sophisticated systems for music, film and video performance are on hand.

When the order "Launch Angels" is given, the girls on stand-by immediately take up their positions on their special cockpit seats, situated in the inner wall, and are hydraulically lifted to their aircraft on Cloudbase's flight deck - and Spectrum becomes Green - for Go!

SPECTRUM ANGEL

VEHICLES

AIRCRAFT

Estimated speed: 3,000 mph
Length: 18.28 metres
Wing span: 10.66 metres
Weight: 18,189 kilos
Engines: Twin turbo jet compressors (exact spec. classified)
Armaments: Air to air missiles, forward cannon

The Angel aircraft is a single seater strike aircraft developed by International Engineering from the World Air Force "Viper" jet, but the exact specifications of its complex control systems and panel remain on the secret list.

Mammoth fuel tanks enable the Angel aircraft to complete any mission without refuelling. Entry to the cockpit is by hydraulic lift from the Amber Room up through the hull of the craft.

Instruments and gunsights are arranged within easy reach of the pilot who has all-round visibility. Behind the pilot's seat is the flight computer and auto-pilot.

The twin-turbo jet compressors serve the rear ram jet. For emergencies, small powerful retro rockets are fitted.

Hyper-sensitive instruments are housed in the nose probe to detect air and metal temperature and wind speeds. Radar and radio equipment is also housed in the nose probe.

The cannons fire computer pre-selected tracer, armour-piercing or rocket shells.

SPECTRUM

PERSONNEL

NAME:
LIEUTENANT GREEN

Real name Seymour Griffiths, Lieutenant Green is the eldest of a family of nine children. Born 18 January, 2041 in Port of Spain, Trinidad, Seymour learnt the hard way! When he was twelve, his parents were killed in an air disaster, leaving him to bring up the family.

Seymour realised to survive, the family must organise. Sharing household chores, the three older brothers and two sisters took it in turns to care for the three babies. Griffiths himself dealt with the welfare authorities who were determined to disperse the family among different foster homes.

His success in keeping his family united is a measure of the courage and determination that found such expression in later life.

Working in various jobs during the day, to earn enough money to keep the family, Seymour attended night education classes at the local high school and later at Kingston University, Jamaica. He gained degrees in music, telecommunications and technology.

As soon as his brothers were able to fend for themselves, Griffiths enrolled in the World Aquanaut Security Patrol as a hydrophone operator. After an advanced course in communications and computer studies, WASP promoted him i/c Marineville Control Tower. He was an obvious choice for Spectrum when the selection Board sought a communications chief.

Full of fun and inclined to be boisterous off duty, Lieutenant Green delights his Spectrum colleagues with his guitar playing.

LIEUTENANT SEPIA AND GOLD, ATTACHED TO SPECTRUM NORTH AFRICAN SECTOR, RELAX DURING AN OFF DUTY PERIOD...

SIX TO FOUR I COME UP WITH THE BIGGEST CATCH.

YOU'RE ON!

MINUTES PASS AS THE TWO MEN TWIST AND TURN EFFORTLESSLY THROUGH THE MARINE GROWTH, THEN...

THE HARPOON CATCHES THE SHARK IN THE SIDE...

GOLD'S WARNING IS UNSEEN, AND DISASTER FOLLOWS...

THE SHARK TURNS IN RETALIATION... DEADLY COMBAT FOLLOWS...

THIS IS THE VOICE OF THE MYSTERONS WE KNOW YOU CAN HEAR US

34

IT IS LIEUTENANT SEPIA WHO REPLIES...

I WILL, SIR!

OBVIOUSLY SPECTRUM NORTH AFRICA IS WELL ORGANISED.

THE CONVOY MOVES OFF...

AND ARRIVES AT THE AIRPORT.

I'LL DRIVE BACK IN THE MSV, GOLD.

SORRY ORDERS ARE THAT I DO!

AND I'M COUNTERMANDING THOSE ORDERS.

UNSEEN SEPIA CLIMBS INTO THE MSV...

WE'RE ESCORTING YOU RIGHT THROUGH TO MADRID, MR. PRESIDENT.

I APPRECIATE IT, GENTLEMEN!

AS THE THREE MEN BOARD THE SPECTRUM PASSENGER JET, THE MSV MAKES A TIGHT TURN AND DRIVES AWAY...

AFTER TAKE OFF SCARLET REMAINS THOUGHTFULLY SILENT UNTIL THE DISTANT SLOPE OF THE COLOSSAL GIBRALTAR BRIDGE COMES INTO VIEW, THEN . . .

WE'VE BEEN TRICKED! THE MYSTERONS THREATENED TO DESTROY THE PRESIDENT WHEN THE GIBRALTAR BRIDGE IS BLOWN UP. WE SAVED THE PRESIDENT, BUT THE BRIDGE IS REALLY WHAT THEY'RE AFTER.

THIS IS THE VOICE OF THE MYSTERONS

WE KNOW YOU CAN HEAR

HOW MUCH DO YOU KNOW ABOUT
SPECTRUM?

Here is a special challenge to see how much you know about the Spectrum Organisation. All the questions are generated from copy found in this book. The answers are on page 45, but see if you can complete the quiz without peeking.

1. Who is the communications officer for Spectrum?
2. What is his real name and where was he born?
3. Who are the Angels?
4. What are their nationalities and real names?
5. Can you name four of the Spectrum agents, giving both code names and real names?
6. From which World Government service did Captain Grey come?
7. Who is Charles Gray and what is his position in Spectrum?
8. Captain Scarlet has been under Mysteron control. What were the ultimate effects of this?
9. What was Captain Magenta's former trader before Spectrum?
10. Why was Magenta recruited?
11. What have all the Spectrum agents in common?
12. Which planet did the Mysterons land on and colonise?
13. The Mysterons have an Earth-based agent, who is he?
14. What are the Mysteron aims?
15. Who or what controls them?
16. What unique power have the Mysterons got?
17. What was Spectrum's former role?
18. What is the name of its headquarters, and where was it built?
19. What is Spectrum's function now?
20. How are Spectrum agents coded?

39

SPECTRUM

PERSONNEL

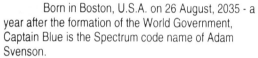

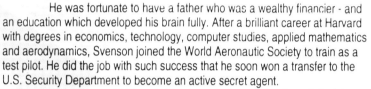

NAME:
CAPTAIN BLUE

Born in Boston, U.S.A. on 26 August, 2035 - a year after the formation of the World Government, Captain Blue is the Spectrum code name of Adam Svenson.

He was fortunate to have a father who was a wealthy financier - and an education which developed his brain fully. After a brilliant career at Harvard with degrees in economics, technology, computer studies, applied mathematics and aerodynamics, Svenson joined the World Aeronautic Society to train as a test pilot. He did the job with such success that he soon won a transfer to the U.S. Security Department to become an active secret agent.

With a force of 20 hand picked agents, he set about revolutionising his command in Eastern Europe - with such success that Bereznik, the breakaway dictatorship opposed to the World Government took exception to the improvements and on three separate occasions attempted to kill him. Each time Svenson managed, by ingenuity and quick thinking, to save himself. But times were changing - the need for a super security force was at hand and Spectrum was formed. It needed agents - and Adam Svenson was among the first chosen.

Off duty he is a keen athlete whose main hobbies are deep sea diving and water skiing.

NAME:
CAPTAIN OCHRE

Another American agent, Captain Ochre, real name Richard Fraser, was born in Detroit, U.S.A. on 23 February, 2035.

Unlike the other agents, Ochre does not have outstanding academic qualifications. Hating High School work, he spent valuable studying time designing and building model aircraft. He learnt to fly at the age of 16, but did not have the degrees to join the World Air Force. Instead he became a member of the World Government Police Corps.

Promotion followed rapidly and he established himself as a brilliant detective. When the Supreme Commander of the WGPC retired, Ochre was in line for the job. But Spectrum also knocked at his door, and the challenge of action made him decide to accept activity over a safe desk job.

SPECTRUM HELICOPTER

VEHICLES

Length:	**13.70 metres**
Blades:	**6 metres**
Seating capacity:	**5**
Estimated speed:	**302 mph**
Weight:	**17,236.8 kilos**
Power plant:	**Air-feed turbos**
Armaments:	**High speed cannon projecting high explosive rockets**

The Spectrum helicopter was designed primarily for high speed transportation of Spectrum personnel over short distances, particularly where rough and difficult terrain is involved. Rugged in design, the helicopter can land on any area its own size, on any surface, and is largely unaffected by air turbulence.

This invaluable stability is provided by the smooth but complex airflow surfaces, and the superb overall balance of design. The wide diameter rotor blades are driven by twin air-induction turbo-jets housed immediately beneath, and above the cabin.

One of the complex controls incorporated in the pilot's control panel is the latest version of a visual navigation aid, first introduced in the mid-twentieth century. Known as the omni-scanner, it consists of a screen showing the terrain over which the 'copter is flying, and enables the pilot to pin-point the position of all Spectrum agents outside Cloudbase.

Although principally a non-combat vehicle, the Spectrum helicopter has a defence armament capable of dealing with all but the strongest opposition.

SPECTRUM PERSONNEL

NAME: CAPTAIN GREY

Code named Captain Grey, Bradley Holden is the real name of this Spectrum agent who was born in Chicago on 4 March, 2033. Educated at the World Naval Academy at San Diego, Grey gained degrees in navigation, aqua-technology and computer studies. On graduating, he immediately enrolled in the submarine service attached to the World Navy and was stationed at Sydney, Australia.

With the coming of the World Aquanaut Security Patrol, Grey was transferred and promoted to Security Commander of this new organisation. He was put in charge of the prototype submarine vessel which was later to become Stingray. In command of this sleek craft, he was a true credit to WASP and his daring campaigns against the threatening underwater enemies have been matched only by Captain Troy Tempest.

Spectrum decided he was an excellent candidate for its elite team of agents and Holden had no hesitation in accepting. Captain Grey is dedicated to his hobby - swimming and the development of aqualung diving gear.

NAME: CAPTAIN MAGENTA

Born in Dublin, Ireland, 17 May, 2034, and given the name Patrick Donaghue. An unusual candidate for the job as Spectrum agent, Captain Magenta came from the criminal fraternity.

When he was three, his parents emigrated to America, settling in a very poor New York suburb. Magenta grew up in an atmosphere of poverty and crime, where learning to become a pick-pocket was more important than learning to read and write.

Encouraged by his mother, however, he worked hard at the local High School and won a scholarship to Yale University. Graduating with degrees in physics, electrical engineering and technology, he joined a Brooklyn firm as a computer programmer, but the boring routine of his job made him long for the life of high adventure, action and big money.

So Magenta turned to crime. Within two years he was controlling many of New York's crime organisations. The Spectrum selection committee realised they would need a man like Magenta, someone who could apply his special talents to a more worthy cause. The new challenge interested Magenta and he was granted a free pardon by the World Government and joined Spectrum.

SPECTRUM SPJ

VEHICLES

PASSENGER JET

Seating capacity:	7 persons		
Crew:	2		
Estimated speed:	1,125 mph		
Range:	12,000 miles		
Length:	23.77 metres	**Weight:**	285,908 kilos
Wing span:	11.27 metres	**Power unit:**	Twin re-heat turbo jets

Designed specially for Spectrum, the S.P.J. provides fast transport for Spectrum agents and their equipment. The roomy cabin can be quickly and easily converted to a VIP lounge, cinema or conference room as readily as a personnel carrier.

The jet carries no armaments, and is normally escorted on dangerous missions by the Angels. Nose stabilising fins are fitted for rarefied air conditions, Cloudbase landings, and supersonic flight.

It is possible to fly the aircraft with a one man crew, the sophisticated flight computer taking the place of the co-pilot/navigator. The main induction plant is fitted to the twin re-heat turbo jet engines for retro-braking.

The rear wing assembly turns through 90 degrees to act as an airbrake when landing.

With a seating capacity of seven, and its versatile interior, the S.P.J., though basically a non-combat vehicle, is used for transporting to Cloudbase executives on official business, and general ferrying chores. In short, the S.P.J. is Spectrum's work-horse!

WE, THE MYSTERONS,

Continued from page 29

The helicopter drew away and was soon lost from sight.

It had been seen from the upper deck, and faces peered down from the rail towards Scarlet. He had now released his hands from their magnetic pads and was using a blow-torch to cut open the frame of the port hole.

It took only seconds, and Captain Scarlet began to scramble through the opening.

Two of the convicts on the upper deck ran shouting to others. There was disbelief and argument among the men on the deck.

The convicts had no leader, and no knowledge of the more intricate workings of the platform. It was some time before they realised that the intruder had broken into the navigation systems room.

They rushed to the lowest deck in a pack and hammered on the door. It was sealed. Captain Scarlet had fused the door to the jambs with quick dabs of his blow-torch.

He had already cut half of a large circle in the floor and removed a few of the deck plates to reveal a couple of large metal ribs and the outer hull plates.

The pounding of fists on the door changed to the clang of hammers and tools. Captain Scarlet worked on. He cut through the hull plates and glimpsed the moving waves below. A great disc of metal fell into the sea.

Scarlet clutched at one of the computer cabinets which controlled the navigation of the huge raft, and dragged it towards the hole. Wires and a cable connecting it to other units stretched. The cabinet toppled through the hole. The cable snapped with a flash and the grey box fell fifty feet towards the water. Other cabinets followed in rapid succession, plunging into the turbulent sea.

"Now," thought the Captain, "this platform can drift uncontrolled on the wide ocean, giving the authorities time to put a force on board to restore order."

He smiled, stepped through the hole himself, and hit the waves just over a second later.

Scarlet floated for half a minute, his survival suit keeping out the biting cold of the water. He looked up as the great shadow of the platform passed away from him, and the beating rotors of the helicopter took its place.

Two minutes later he was back in the flying machine beside Captain Blue. The machine soared high away from the waves, and to the east there was the dark heavy line of the American continent.

"I didn't realise we were so close to land," said Captain Scarlet.

"The platform was travelling at a steady twenty-five knots all the time you were aboard," replied Blue. "And within another hour it will run aground at Los Toros Bay. I've just heard a Navy report that the platform is now caught up in an in-shore current. Those convicts will make landfall now, in spite of what you have done."

Captain Scarlet looked grim. "And at least one of them has been Mysteronised," he said. "But what else could we do. Let's hope he can be spotted and eliminated before he causes more trouble."

"Yes," agreed Blue. "You've managed to give the authorities time to organise a reception committee for the prisoners. There's still a chance we can foil the Mysteron plan."

"Maybe," nodded Scarlet. "It will be touch and go whether all those desperate men can be captured." He sighed deeply. "When are we ever going to defeat the Mysterons?" he asked in frustration.

That was one question that only the future could answer...if there was to be a future for Earth!

QUIZ ANSWERS

1. Lieutenant Green.
2. Seymour Griffiths.
3. Five female pilots who command the Spectrum strike force. Their names are Harmony, Destiny, Symphony, Rhapsody and Melody.
4. Melody...Magnolia Jones, American. Destiny...Juliette Pontoin, French. Harmony...Chan Kwan, Japanese. Rhapsody...Dianne Simms, British. Symphony...Karen Wainwright, American.
5. Captain Scarlet - Paul Metcalfe. Captain Blue - Adam Svenson. Captain Grey - Bradley Holden. Captain Magenta - Patrick Donaghue. Captain Ochre -

Richard Fraser.
6. World Navy and World Aeronautic Society.
7. Charles Gray is Colonel White, supreme commander-in-chief of Spectrum.
8. The effects made him indestructible.
9. He was head of a crime syndicate.
10. Because Spectrum needed an agent who could move freely in the underworld and had numerous criminal contacts.
11. They have all specialised in one field of activity and are cool headed, quick thinking and able to react quickly in tough situations.
12. Mars
13. Captain Black
14. The complete destruction of Earth.
15. They are controlled by computers.
16. The power of reconstructing dead beings and objects that have been destroyed.
17. A specialised World Security force.
18. Cloudbase. It was constructed partly in Sweden and partly in outer space.
19. To combat the Mysterons' threat to destroy the world.
20. They are coded by colours, Scarlet, Blue, Ochre, etc.

45

WE THE MYSTERONS WILL DESTROY THE ALPINE TOUR COACH!

A luxury coach on an Alpine Tour has been Mysteronised. It is heading for a mountain pass where it will almost certainly crash over the edge. Starting at Cloudbase, select which agent you are going to be and follow the course undertaken by Spectrum. See how quickly you can reach the passengers.

The game can be played by one or more players. You must follow the instructions shown.

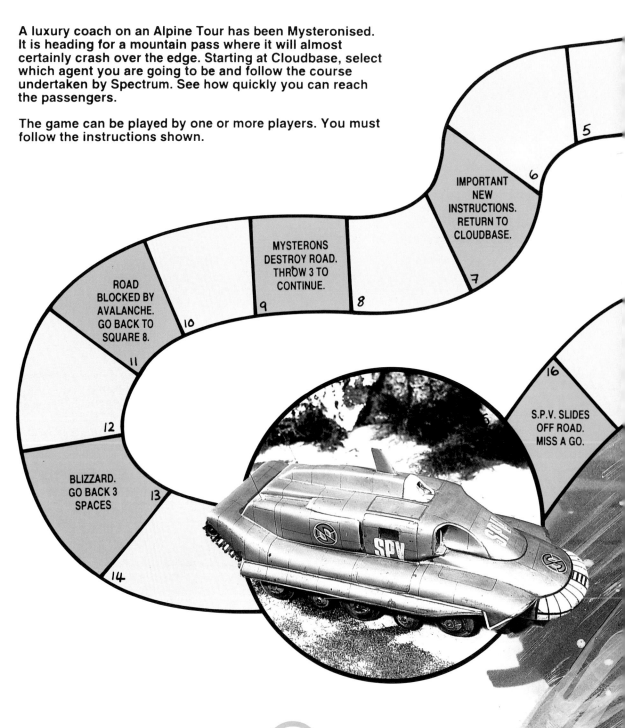

5

6

IMPORTANT NEW INSTRUCTIONS. RETURN TO CLOUDBASE.

7

MYSTERONS DESTROY ROAD. THROW 3 TO CONTINUE.

9

8

ROAD BLOCKED BY AVALANCHE. GO BACK TO SQUARE 8.

10

11

16

S.P.V. SLIDES OFF ROAD. MISS A GO.

12

BLIZZARD. GO BACK 3 SPACES

13

14